The Stable
Where Jesus
Was Born

by RHONDA GOWLER GREENE

illustrated by SUSAN GABER

ATHENEUM BOOKS *for* YOUNG READERS
NEW YORK LONDON TORONTO SYDNEY

Atheneum Books for Young Readers
An imprint of Simon & Schuster Children's Publishing Division
1230 Avenue of the Americas
New York, New York 10020

Book design by Michael Nelson
The text of this book is set in Guardi Roman.
The illustrations are rendered in acrylic on Bristol board.

Manufactured in China
First edition
2 4 6 8 10 9 7 5 3 1

Library of Congress Cataloging-in-Publication Data
Greene, Rhonda Gowler.
The stable where Jesus was born / Rhonda Gowler Greene ; illustrated by
Susan Gaber.—1st ed.
p.   cm.
Originally published: New York:
Atheneum Books for Young Readers, c1999.
ISBN-13: 978-1-4169-5048-6
ISBN-10: 1-4169-5048-6
1. Jesus Christ—Nativity—Juvenile literature. I. Gaber, Susan. II. Title.
BT315.3.G74 2007
232.92—dc22   2007002581

For Matt
⁓ R. G. G.

To Joanne
⁓ S. G.

This is the stable where Jesus was born.

⚜

This is the cow in the sweet-smelling hay,
the cat and her kittens and three mice at play,
that lived in the stable where Jesus was born.

⚜

This is the mother, Mary by name,
the mother of Jesus she became,
who sat near the cow in the sweet-smelling hay.

This is the father, Joseph, so tall,
who cared for the baby and animals all,
but mostly the mother, Mary by name.

These are the shepherds who came in the night,
who left flocks of sheep in their hurry and flight
and wished well the father, Joseph, so tall.

This is the angel who said, "Fear not!"
who spoke of a birth in a glorious spot
and sent fast the shepherds who came in the night.

This is the town called Bethlehem
where families gathered and filled every inn,
beheld by the angel who said, "Fear not!"

This is the earth all round and bright
that glimmered with hope that first Christmas night
at news from a town called Bethlehem.

This is the baby in swaddling clothes,
the small precious baby, the one whom God chose
to come to the earth all round and bright
that glimmered with hope that first Christmas night

at news from a town called Bethlehem
where families gathered and filled every inn,

beheld by the angel who said, "Fear not!"
who spoke of a birth in a glorious spot

and sent fast the shepherds who came in the night,
who left flocks of sheep in their hurry and flight

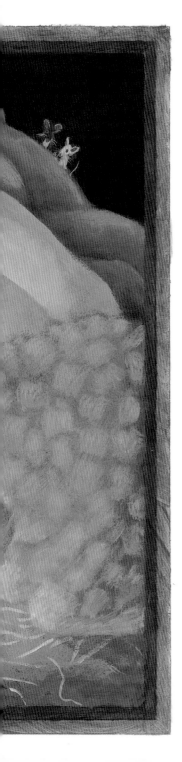

and wished well the father, Joseph, so tall,

who cared for the baby and animals all,

⚜

but mostly the mother, Mary by name,
the mother of Jesus she became,

⚜

who sat near the cow in the sweet-smelling hay,
the cat and her kittens and three mice at play,